Case of the Missing Dog

GREGORY GRANT

Ordering Information:

Prime Seven Media
518 Landmann St.
Tomah City, WI 54660

Printed in the United States of America

Case of the Missing Dog

Let me introduce myself. My name is Greg and my dog is Jake,

My dog and I live with my parents Bill and Marge. One day we heard that there was a dog napper in the neighborhood. My friend Grego said to me that I had better keep an eye out for Jake when he is outside which I said that I would.

The day after I was out in the front yard doing some gardening and Jake was helping by sniffing around when this hobo boy came down the street and started talking to me and playing with Jake. He said, "I once had a dog but it ran away and we never found him again". Suddenly the phone rang, I rushed inside thinking that Jake would follow me like he usually does. I answered the phone and it was a friend of mine so we talked for about 5 minutes then I went back outside thinking Jake had gone around the back. I didn't think twice about him and got back to work, then it dawned on me that I hadn't seen or heard of Jake, so I called for him 'Jake, Jake'. There was no answer so I whistled for him 'wee, wee'. Still no answer. I was getting worried, which is not unusual for me so I said to myself "I'll wait five minutes more and if he doesn't come I'll give to police a ring".

Five minutes went by very slowly and Jake still didn't return, so I said very loudly 'OK I AM CALLING THE COPS!' Which I did but all the police said, "well what do you want us to do about it? It really is a RSPCA matter". I called the RSPCA and they said, " Well Sir give us details of what your dog looks like and we will start searching for it. If we find it we will call you". With that I put the phone down and hoped for the best, but that hobo boy came to mind and I wondered to myself whether he was up to no good with Jake so I went back outside where we were talking and lo and behold on the ground was Jake's dog tags.

I rushed back inside to call back the RSPCA to say I thought he had been dognapped. They asked me how I knew and I told them that his dog tags were on the ground. They told me it was now a police matter, so I hung up and called the police to tell them. They said, "Ok give us his details and someone will be around to talk to you." I told them where I lived and within five minutes they were around. I described Jake giving them a picture, and told them he was microchipped and they told me that this bloke normally dechips them, so it would be hard to find the dog. They said they would do their best. They also asked me what the hobo looked like and I said, "Well he was wearing a purple tracksuit pants and yellow hood jacket with sunglasses" which I thought was strange because it was raining. The police then said, "Well it fits the description we got from other dog nap victims" and on the way out they said "Well Sir we'll be on the look out for him". On that note they got in their police car and left. A couple of days later I got this mysterious phone call saying that if I didn't hand over 1 million dollars he would give my dog up for stir fry. I said 'oh no' He said '"Meet me in Rome outside the Trevi Fountain by Thursday at 12pm UK time and don't call the police or your dog will get it."

I booked a ticket to Rome and got there on Wednesday so I could tell the local police there as he didn't tell me not to tell the Rome police. The Rome police rang up the Melbourne police and while they were doing this I decided to take in a few sights, since I had never been overseas before. Me being a church goer I thought I would go to St. Peter's church and have a look around. I saw the Swiss Guard, guarding the entrance and I said Gee Whiz. It was so big, with a high dome and many statues and pictures of the past popes.

After seeing St. Peter's. I walked on to the Coliseum. I had heard that this was where they used to fight in Roman days; I thought how could they fight like that. There were underground tunnels and it was great to see. "Well I better get to the hotel now as tomorrow is the day I have to met hobo." The Police said to me that I should go and meet this hobo boy and give him the money, which I had to borrow. The next day came and I was waiting outside the fountain at 12 noon.

Prompt at noon, he came along but before I gave him my money I asked, "now where is my dog?" "You will not get your dog from me as I am only the messenger for someone else." "Who" I said. He said he didn't know so I got mad and hit him. The police saw this and came running to find out what the problem was, so I told them that he stole my dog in Australia and for some reason had brought it here, so they took us both in to talk about it.

When we got to the police station, the police questioned the man about where he had taken the dog but he answered "Well sirs I was only told to kidnap the dog and take it to Rome." He told me to catch a plane to Buckingham Palace in London, so it looked like I was off to England to see the Queen. The Rome police said I should go to London and they would call ahead and tell the London Bill my story and ask them to help me.

Several hours later I touched down at Heathrow airport, where I met the Bill and they filled me in that I was looking for a man wearing a pink tracksuit with curly hair wearing yellow sunglasses and he would try to contact me by phone. At 5:00pm London time the public phone rang next to where I was having a bite to eat. It was a man calling himself 'The One' telling me to meet him in front of Buckingham Palace the next day at 12 noon with the money, which I had taken back from the hobo. That night I had a bad night's sleep, because on the plane over I heard a news report saying how robbers stole a safe full of diamonds on Friday, in Melbourne the same day that hobo took Jake and I wondered if it was connected. I was thinking all night about it.

The next day came but before I went to the Palace, I wanted to see Trafalgar Square, it was a pretty sight.

Now I will get to the Palace. 12 noon came and I arrived at the Buckingham Palace and sat on a stonewall around the Queen Victoria Memorial. When this man with curly hair came along wearing a pink tracksuit and yellow sunglasses and he came up to me and saying, "Hello, my name is The One. Are you Greg?" and I said 'yes' and he said, "Have you got the money?" "First where is my dog?" I asked "I'll tell you when you give me the money". I was getting angry with him so I refused to give him the money and as the Bill were around, I screamed to make a scene, so the Bill came in and arrested us and took us both back the station.

He said very stubbornly that he was only a messenger and was told to get the money from the guy that was in Rome and fly over to Innsbruck and go to the Alps where there is a man with a St. Bernard. He is the next person to contact about the dog.

So I got back on the plane and flew to Innsbruck where I met the Innsbruck police and they told me what was going on. They got me a room at the local hotel and arranged for me to catch the train to the Alps to meet this guy the next day.

So tomorrow came very quickly and a person met me at the hotel saying that she would come with me and pick the guy up while I carried on. So off we went up the Alps and when we got there he was very noticeable because he was the only man with a dog there. I went up to him and introduced myself and we talked but he refused to tell me where Jake was so I made a snow ball and threw it at him. He then grabbed me and on that signal my female champion came in and took him away to the Innsbruck station. There he got lights shone on his face and soap stuffed in his mouth until he gave up and told us that he was meant to meet another guy in Venice whose name was 'the singer' as he sings on the gondolas.

So off to Venice to meet a Gondolier who I should know when I meet him. I arrived in Venice at 11pm that night and the guards met me and took me to a hotel room were I got ready for bed. The next day sharp on 6.a.m I got up and got ready to go down to the foyer to meet the guards again and they helped me by taking me to where the gondolas float. It wasn't hard because Venice is a small city on the water. I recognized the man they call the "Singer" for he was the only one there.

I got in the gondola and asked him his name he said, "I am the Singer." "Where is The One with my 1 million dollars?" I said "I am he but where is my dog?" He said, "The dog is in Italy at the Leaning tower of Pisa". I pushed him into the water.

I got back on the plane this time to Italy where I was looking for a man with a camera. When I got there, I met one man there. He was a policeman and I said "Only one?" and he said "yes the rest are busy" so I said "come on." On the way we stopped at Florence and saw the famous statue of David by Michel Angelo. When we got to the Leaning Tower of Pisa, we looked for this man with a camera. When we found him he wanted his million dollars before he said anything and I point blank refused. So we argued he tried to flee the scene but my friend caught him and took him back to the Leaning Tower of Pisa to question him, mainly because the police station had burnt down last year and they were rebuilding it. He said that I would find my dog tied up in the backyard of the clog maker named Hans in Holland.

Once again I got on a plane bound for Holland where I was to meet a clog maker by the name of Hans. When I got to Holland there was no one to meet me so I was on my own for this one. I went to where they made clogs and walked into the factory to ask for the clog maker Hans. The other worker knew him and they pointed him out to me. When I went up to him and asked for the dog, he acted like he didn't know of any dog, so I backed him into a corner and asked him again. He was shaking and said "the dog is out the back. Now where's my millions dollars?" "You don't get anything at all," I said and he tried to run for it but tripped over my shoe and hit his head.

After I checked if he was alright, I went to the back yard and there was Jake lying out to it and got out of there before the police arrived. I was a block away when I saw the police van pull up and raid the joint. I was still wondering if the big diamonds theft that was in Australia had anything to do with what had happened so I got Jake to the Vet. They did a thorough test and found a bag diamonds in his stomach. Obviously he ate them when hobo was playing with him. They put Jake under and took out the diamonds, and I went to the police the same day explaining what had happened and gave them the diamonds. They said that they had been following the news and my dog and me were on it. On the way home I decided to detour via the USA. where we had a look at Disney Land.

Jake and I then went back to Australia. That was one a trip, I never thought I would have.

Written by Greg Grant

©2007